The truth of the heart is written in the stars...

Conall Blair is the son of Gray Vale's Alpha, but he'd rather be a thorn in the side of the neighboring Stoke Ridge pack. For him, peace and harmony are little better than death—in all aspects of life, even relationships.

Zoltan Valenta, heir of Stoke Ridge, is a man of duty who's suddenly having doubts. Though his father has arranged his marriage to Fiona Blair, Zoltan can't shake his fascination with her twin brother, Conall.

When the two men find themselves unwittingly pushed together, there's no denying the heat between them. Against all rules, expectations and commitments, can they really just yield to the hand fate deals them?

Sale of this book without a front cover may be unauthorized. If this book is coverless, it may have been reported to the publisher as "unsold or destroyed" and neither the author nor the publisher may have received payment for it.

No part of this book may be adapted, stored, copied, reproduced or transmitted in any form or by any means, electronic or mechanical, including photocopying, recording, or by any information storage and retrieval system, without permission in writing from the publisher.

Thank you for respecting the hard work of this author.

His Fated Mate
Gray Vale Pack
Book One

Copyright © 2021 Evie Riley
Second Edition
ISBN: 978-1-77357-689-3

Naughty Nights Press LLC
Cover Art By Willsin Rowe

Names, characters and incidents depicted in this book are products of the author's imagination or are used fictitiously. Any resemblance to actual events, locales, organizations, or persons, living or dead, is entirely coincidental and beyond the intent of the author.

HIS FATED MATE

GRAY VALE PACK

BOOK ONE

EVIE RILEY

CHAPTER ONE

CONALL

THE FOREST AROUND us radiated life. I drank it in through nose and ears, but there was so more to it than that. My wolf growled inside me, sensing prey.

The feeling was so strong that even my human side itched for action. Any excuse to shift would be fine by me. Patrolling this disputed region between our lands and Stoke Ridge only tossed me a little excitement once in a while, but today felt rich with potential.

Glen came up beside me. The prickling of energy coming off him only got me even more keyed up.

"Deer," I murmured.

"Duh," Glen replied. "You're not the only one with a fuckin' nose, Connie."

I reached out and slapped the back of his head without even looking. "What've I told you about calling me that?"

Glen let out a low growl. "Used to let me."

"That was when I was also fucking you. You see the connection there, dude?"

Immediately, our attention flew across to the clearing, and the big buck that crept into sight.

Glen slid his rifle down off his

shoulder, but I stopped him.

"Uh-uh. We do it like nature intended."

"Ugh, seriously? That's one thing I definitely don't miss about you."

I stripped off in seconds, fending away Glen's lustful glare as I did. We'd had our chance, and it didn't work out. If he couldn't get over it then he was no good as a member of my patrol.

He kept his voice low and deep. "Why do you even come out with us lowly shit-kickers, anyway, Conall? You have options guys like me could never even dream of."

"You call going to fancy-pants shindigs and week-long meetings *options*? That's not me, bro. Besides, in three days, my sister is taking the fall for all of us."

That was the biggest downside to being what amounted to pack royalty. Marriages and matings that were all about strategy. Thankfully, that shit didn't apply to me. Only hetero pairings were recognized, still.

Because of all that, my twin, Fiona, was gonna be all hitched up to the pristine, primped and puckered heir of the Stoke Ridge Pack, Zoltan Valenta. And all for the lamest of reasons.

Peace.

More like death, as I saw it. If we couldn't get into harmless little pissing contests with our snobbish neighbors, then what the hell was the good of being wolves? Life is conflict, and vice versa.

I glanced across at Glen. "You're still dressed."

"C'mon, Con. You know how your father is."

Yeah, I knew. He treated shifting like it

was a religious ceremony. Just like the ancient ones had. Tradition was everything in wolf packs.

"Dude, if my father's fancy notions mattered to me, I wouldn't be out here with you lowly shit-kickers, now. Would I? I'd be lying back on a fucking velvet sofa with servant boys feeding me grapes."

Glen made a quiet scoffing sound and worked his clothes off. "Let's just fucking get this done, so I don't have to hear any more shit."

I shook my head with a wry smile. "Do you even shift, bro?"

Before he'd finished rolling his eyes, I opened myself up to the wolf, letting it ignite within me. Shifting was like sex. No matter how many times I did it, I always wanted more.

My body jolted, my muscles and bones

danced around each other, and then it was done. I didn't even wait for Glen. The scent of that buck was too fucking delicious.

I crept forward, keeping low. The buck was spooked already. It was a buzz in the air that brought his scent with it. Twenty feet. Fifteen. His big body quivered and he cast his head around. No need to run this guy down. He was so close I could almost taste him.

As I tensed to spring at my prey, a rifle shot rang out. The assault of noise had me flinching away, and a second later the buck dropped dead.

I'd been so close. Glen was gonna pay for that. Robbing my wolf of his succor. In my rage, I shifted back, ready to tear my cohort a new one.

Before I could turn around, three men

in Stoke Ridge uniforms moved into the clearing from the far side. One of them carrying a rifle, all of them pleased with themselves. Obviously new recruits, or they'd be treading a lot more carefully.

I marched forward, more than ready to turn my anger on them. I sensed, rather than saw, Glen moving into position behind me.

"Hey! You fuckin' Stoke Ridge assholes."

All three of the other side's patrolmen tensed as we moved closer. "Back down, Gray Vale. It's our trophy."

"Not when you bag it on our land."

Rifle dude sneered at me. "Well, when we bag one on your land, pal, we'll be sure to let you know. But this here is Stoke Ridge land."

I took a cleansing breath. As much as

EVIE RILEY

I'd been looking forward to taking down that buck, that would have been little more than an appetizer. This here was main course and dessert, all rolled into one. There was nothing I liked quite so much as tussling with these hoity-toity Ridgers.

"Is that right?"

"You know it is, grunt. Now, run off back to your kennels." He flicked his eyes down for a split second and then back up. "And tuck that tail of yours between your legs."

I gave the guy a flash of teeth. "Or maybe you want that... *tail*... right between *your* legs, Ridgy. I see how you look at me."

For me, that was just a throwaway comment. But for a Ridgy, it was the ultimate slur. Stoke Ridge society was stuck in the fucking nineteenth century when it came to sexuality.

Okay, a taunt like that one was low-hanging fruit, but all I wanted was for them to make the first move. The fact it worked so well every single time only meant I'd keep using it again and again.

Rifle dude snarled and handed his weapon to his right hand man. I went into a crouch, arms out, waiting.

The guy burst forward, charging straight for me. Like a fucking amateur. I let him slam into me, chest to chest, before spinning on the spot and throwing him halfway across the clearing. He landed in a sprawling mess of limbs.

"Now, you guys stand down," I said, letting all my menace and breeding come bubbling out in my voice. It did no good, though. These guys were young, dumb

EVIE RILEY

and full of... themselves.

The rifle guy sprang up to a squat, baring his teeth, which were growing longer.

I raised one eyebrow. "You gonna take this down to wolf level, kid?" That was the other thing with Stoke Ridge. They were even more stuffy about shifting than my father was. "'Cause I spend half my life there. Do you?"

That gentle little reminder seemed to do the trick, and he came back up onto his feet. When he approached me this time, he showed a ton more caution. Still not enough, though.

He threw a wild punch that couldn't have been more telegraphed. It was like a movie punch. He spent so much time pulling his arm back I could have made a coffee while I waited for him to throw it.

HIS FATED MATE

I pulled my head back and let his fist fly past, then wrapped my hands around the back of his head and neck, throwing him into the scrub and dirt face first.

No other man had even moved yet. Glen leaned back on a tree, stifling a yawn. The Stoke Ridge guys looked wide eyed and shell shocked. I already knew they were green, but I wouldn't mind betting this was their first ever patrol. That'd explain why they were so cavalier about taking down the buck on disputed lands.

As the main Ridgy came back up onto his feet, I held my hands up for calm. "Give it up, dude. Take your lumps and head back home."

"I'll take my lumps. And my trophy."

"No, you'll be leaving the buck." I crossed my arms and narrowed my eyes.

EVIE RILEY

"Understood?"

I could see a thousand different words bubbling up in his head. Some of them were punching so hard at his pride he almost said them.

"All right," he ground out. "But you understand *this*... I'm not backing down."

"No? It kinda looks like you are."

"Well, unlike you peasants, we here in Stoke Ridge value tradition. So, I'm allowing this to pass, for the sake of the upcoming wedding." He took his rifle back from his cohort and curled his lip. "You... do know about the wedding, right?"

"Of course he does," Glen interrupted. "He's—"

"I'm not interested in it. Perky prince Zoltan is lucky we're letting him into our pack at all."

The other guy tensed all over. I wasn't

even sure he realized he'd tightened his grip on the weapon. "Let's be clear, you ass. It's your woman who's being elevated here. You and your caretaker Alpha should get on your knees and thank—"

That was as far as he got before my fist hit the side of his face. As much as I loved being wolf, sometimes hands worked better than paws.

The guy dropped like a sack of dirt, and I landed on him just as heavily. My weight on his chest, my hand on his throat.

His two patrolmen froze, their fear filling my nostrils. I'm sure they could sense the battle experience and silent aggression radiating off me, and made the sensible decision to stand down.

"Now it's your turn to listen, sunshine," I growled. "Yeah, Patrick Blair is only a second generation Alpha. If you think that weakens our pack in any way, you're welcome to test your claims."

"Get the hell off me. And for God's sake, cover yourself up."

"You Ridgies are so damn uptight. Never met a bunch of shifters so fuckin' scared of being naked." I rolled my hips just a little. "Or maybe you're scared of how much you're enjoying the view."

"Get off."

As much as I enjoyed roughing up Ridgies, this little scene had passed its sell-by date. There was nothing to be gained anymore. I stood, and offered the guy my hand. He slapped it away and got to his feet at his own speed.

"Lord Valenta will hear of this."

"Lord? You guys are so into this hierarchy shit it's... well, it's fucking embarrassing."

"Whether you accept it or not, every pack is a hierarchy, grunt. And the wrath of your Alpha will come down on you for this."

"It won't be the first time."

They turned and headed back into their territory with a last, narrow-eyed glare at the buck they'd taken down.

As they disappeared into the brush, another of my patrol team came running up from behind.

"Alec," I said. "What's up?"

"Better get dressed, dude. I'm taking your duties from here on. Daddy wants a word with you."

Glen chuckled without any real humor. "Wrath of the Alpha, indeed. News travels fast."

CHAPTER TWO

ZOLTAN

MY FATHER STRUTTED around the grand hall, chest swollen and stride long. Barking orders to staff and craftsmen, deciding on the menu, the decorations, the... I don't know. The ideal temperature for vows to be taken, or something.

It seemed he dedicated his every waking moment to nothing less than my upcoming wedding. He was worse than the most caricatured bridezilla.

"Ah, son," he blustered. "I only wish your mother was still with us. She'd be so proud."

I'd only been four when she drowned, taking my unborn brother with her. Over twenty years had passed, and still the pain sliced me as though it was new.

Father, on the other hand, had simply rolled on with life. That's what generations of Alphas had always done.

I'd watched in disappointed awe, the way he kept on keeping on, barging on with life as though the loss of half one's family was nothing more than a hiccup. But it had planted deep doubts in my own heart.

If he coped so well with their loss, then would it hurt him any deeper were I to

HIS FATED MATE

die? Over the years, I let that thought drive a deeper and wider wedge between us.

Now here we were, at another tipping point. Three days. That was all I had left before I'd be absorbed by the great machine. In marrying this Fiona Blair, I would cease to exist, in a sense. Forgo my identity in order to be one more puzzle piece in the vast history of the Stoke Ridge pack, and the two dozen generations of Valenta ancestors who'd led before me. Nothing more than the latest portrait in the great hall.

Tradition. That's what mattered. I knew, because for as long as I could remember, father made sure to hammer that home with me.

In all honesty, I couldn't tell if I agreed with him or not. In the jumble of

EVIE RILEY

teachings, dogma and lectures that had been drilled into my head all my life, finding an independent thought—a part of myself that was truly mine—was near impossible.

For a thousand years, Valenta men—and *only* men—had presided over this pack. Back in Europe to begin with, and for over two hundred years here in Stoke Ridge. Time moved on, rendering this place little more than an anachronism, yet I truly had no idea how to change things, or what they should change to.

More telling, I had even less idea what was in my own heart. All I knew was what I *didn't* want. Deep down, I didn't want to disappoint my father. Even deeper down, I did *not* want to marry this woman. Or *any* woman. I couldn't yet discern the reason. I simply had no interest in the idea.

HIS FATED MATE

Being the Alpha of a wolf pack was, to me, the antithesis of freedom. We were more bound by customs, rules and *thou-shalt-nots* than any of our pack members. Even those in the military.

The Blairs were new to leadership, but I'd encountered the Alpha many times over the years. His presence was as commanding as my father's, yet in a whole different way.

Father balanced precariously at the top of an ancient tree. He was born to be an Alpha, but had to grow into the role.

Patrick Blair, on the other hand, filled rooms with just his charisma. His face and body bore the kinds of scars my father let others to take in his stead.

I'm sure Blair's daughter would be a formidable and honorable woman, but I'd never met my bride-to-be. As was customary, it was the first born son who'd accompanied Patrick Blair to any joint functions.

Though technically, I'd never met Conall Blair, either. Nor had I even seen him in close to ten years. He'd stopped attending functions in his mid-teens, which had robbed all the light from the experiences from then on. He'd been the one part of the whole rigmarole I'd enjoyed.

With his midnight black hair and his sharp, blue eyes, he'd had me mesmerized from the first instant I'd seen him. It took all my will power to keep from staring at him every time we were sat across from each other.

He'd radiated such intensity that I'd never been game to initiate a conversation. How could I, the latest in an immeasurable line of sheltered nobles, measure up to men like these? Men of action.

Most of my pack looked down their noses at the Blairs, simply because they were so new to leading. But that boy—man, now—possessed the magnetism and charisma an Alpha needed. Perhaps too *much* of it, if that were possible. I knew I'd have done just about anything he told me to... had he ever spoken to me.

That in and of itself was damn troubling. How was I meant to be the Alpha my pack—and father—expected, if I was so ready to kneel before another man?

The arrival of a messenger brought me back into the here and now.

"Lord Valenta."

"What is it? Can't you see we're in the

middle of preparations?"

"There has been another skirmish in the disputed lands, lord. By the description, it's the same troublemaker from Gray Vale as always. Shall we send men to exact reparations?"

"Of course not. We're days from reaching a resolution. I'll deal with it."

"My lord."

The messenger bowed, and I bit into my tongue to keep from laughing. I understood my father's desire for order and hierarchy, but in truth, he'd turned pack leadership into a parody. As if he'd watched too many movies about King Arthur and thought they were documentaries.

The messenger marched out, and my father went back to strutting around and making plans. Plans that felt like a thick blanket wrapping around me, and suddenly I found breathing difficult.

I slipped away unnoticed, desperate for an escape of some kind. I knew my place, and what was expected of me. Yet, there was an aching inside me that could not be assuaged by duty alone.

I made my way down from the main hall and out into the open air. As I came out to the courtyard, I spotted the messenger and called out to him.

He waited obediently as I approached. "Your name?"

"Rogers, sir."

"Tell me, Rogers. This troublemaker…"

"Yes, sir. They say he's as strong as three men, and as ugly as a bear. And he has… unnatural desires." He said the last part with a sour sneer.

"What kind of desires?"

EVIE RILEY

"Sir, they say he—forgive me, sir—he *consorts* only with other men."

I bit down on my tongue. As sinful as the thought of that was, somehow it called my wolf out of his torpor. I'm sure all my beastly half wanted was to bite out the throat of such a wrongdoer. That was the *only* explanation.

"You've encountered him?"

"Thankfully not, sir. He may be just a patrolman, but he has a real hard-on for fucking up our guys." The man gasped as he suddenly remembered who I was. "My deepest apologies for my language, sir."

I waved off his embarrassment. "And this latest encounter? Where was it?"

"In the Bark Gully area, sir."

"Hm. All right then, Rogers. Thank you."

He seemed relieved as I dismissed him

without any comment about his harsh words. My father has always been strict on public decency—as defined by his own standards—and no doubt everybody expected me to react the same way.

I simply couldn't shake the image of this troublemaker from my mind. Though I'd never met him, he'd become an obsession for me through reputation alone.

I closed my eyes and let my mind picture him. My breath became short and sharp again, only this time it was from exhilaration. I couldn't have explained it if I'd been asked to. He was little more than a brigand, yet he seemed to represent all that I'd never experienced. And all that I wondered about.

That was a man who was truly free. No rules, no quarter, no fucks given. Just the thought of him excited me in ways my unseen fiancée never had.

Of course, that was a whole other problem. While there were no laws in place, my pack had always frowned upon anything other than strict one man, one woman partnerships. Married, de facto, whatever.

And the fact was, no woman had ever excited me like this anonymous scoundrel did. If I was to be trapped in a marriage for the rest of my life, I vowed I wouldn't go down without a fight.

I needed to understand what it meant to be truly free before I allowed myself to be locked in to the prison of leadership. My entire pack had sticks up their butts all the damn time. Even our lowest-ranked military guys were all about the rules and propriety.

HIS FATED MATE

What little I knew of Gray Vale led me to believe they were essentially the same.

All except one man. I needed to meet him before I gave up everything that was truly me. And I needed to do it now, before common sense intervened.

CHAPTER THREE

CONALL

THE MEETING WITH my father went pretty much as I'd expected. He hadn't heard about our little squabble with the Ridgies when he summoned me, so the first half was all about how I had to step up and represent at an official level.

Then, he hit me with the news that I'd be acting as best man for Fiona's husband-to-be.

"What the fuck? He doesn't have any brothers or friends?"

"No brothers. No friends of what Anton Valenta calls the *right status*." Father leaned back in his chair. "Besides, I know you, son. This is pretty much the only way I can be sure you'll even attend."

The phone rang just at that moment, and father took the call immediately, while I seethed quietly at his crafty maneuvering.

Glen was right, as it turned out. News really did travel fast. The call was from Anton Valenta, and my father's expression left no doubt the discussion was all about my hijinks out on patrol.

Father made all the usual assurances, and then ended the call, only to give me his standard lecture about winning meaning nothing when the fight was pointless. That it wasn't a requirement of leadership to beat your chest. It was the same speech he always hit me with.

"You could learn a thing or two from your sister, Con."

There was no doubt in my mind he was right about that. Fiona was six minutes younger than I was, but she was all calm, measured control. Though I knew I had to get my shit together, for the sake of the pack, I couldn't escape the truth; that my entire life was still driven by my balls, all day and night.

Still, it felt as if father was ashamed of everything that had brought us to power. With the ending of the previous Alpha's bloodline, the traditional challenge took place, and my grandfather won out. Through strength, resilience, and sheer bloody-minded will. The mark of an Alpha, in my opinion.

Patrick Blair clearly thought that was an idea whose time had passed. I swear, every day, he wanted to be more like those fucking Ridgies, and the way they geek out over rigmarole and ceremony.

Finally, I managed to work my way out of the meeting, after giving him all the assurances that I'd behave myself, and would attend the wedding. He even went down to the nuts and bolts of having me promise to wear a fucking tux.

I ran into Fiona as I left the main hall. As always, the first thing she did was pull me into a hug.

"I heard you've been defending our honor, big brother."

"Is that what I was doing? Dad says I'm making life difficult for everyone."

HIS FATED MATE

"Yeah, well, that *is* kind of your special skill. You even used to elbow me when we were in the womb."

"You were putting your feet on *my* side. I'd clearly drawn a line across the middle."

"Doofus." She eased out of my arms. "But have you ever thought about... oh, I don't know. Acting your age? Playing the part of Alpha's understudy?"

"Ugh. That would require a whole set of special skills I don't even want to think about."

"You mean like *my* kind?"

"I don't know. You claim you can sense mate bonds. Sounds kinda dubious to me."

"That's *one* of my skills. There's a range of others. Importantly, none of them involve poking at the bruises of another pack."

"What fun is there in that?"

She gave me a light punch my shoulder. "So, what's the damage, Con? Bread and water for two weeks?"

"I wish. That I could handle. No, he's taken me off patrol. Says I can't be trusted. You believe that?"

"You want the truth?"

"Of course not."

"Then, uh... let's see. Oh, holy fuck, bro! That's so crazy—"

"Knock it off, asshole."

"You won't be able to call me that when I'm a queen, buddy boy."

I gave her hair a brotherly yank. "Still can't believe you're going through with it. I could never do that."

"Yes, well, you know my thoughts about the different ways men and women make sacrifices for their packs."

I put my hands up in mock surrender. "Please, no more."

"Jerk. But really, I guess I don't mind. All in all, things could be worse. I mean, I've never met him, but I've heard he's crazy good-looking, and a calm and considerate man."

"You got the first part right. Can't really say about the second. But how do *you* know all this?"

"I have a few contacts over there."

"Stoke Ridge?"

"Of course. You throw fists, I throw parties. There's more than one way to be enemies with people, y'know."

Once again, my sister both surprised and inspired me.

We walked in silence for a few seconds, before she spoke again. "Look, the guys

EVIE RILEY

tell me you've been targeting the Ridgies pretty hard the last couple months. What's your problem with them?"

I made a short scoffing sound, hoping that would speak volumes. Of course, it didn't work with Fi. It never had.

"Spill it, bro."

I sighed once for show, then put my arm over Fi's shoulders. "It's a lot of things. But mostly, it boils down to their attitude. They have the high ground and all the game. We have the fertile valley and all the crops. They treat us like peasants."

"It works out in the end. We do a lot of trade with them."

"We're fucking *wolves*, Fi. *Hunters*. We take, we don't trade."

"God, for someone who claims to hate tradition…"

Glen came running up to us before she could finish. "Con, you better come with me."

"Now what?"

"Something to show you."

"I've seen it, bud. It's very nice, but it's not for me anymore."

"Ha ha. C'mon, man."

"Fine." I kissed Fi's forehead. "I'm gonna miss the fuck outta you when you become a Stoke Ridge geek, y'know."

"Oh, but I'll have no problem looking down on you, bro. All the other peasants, too, but *especially* you." She flashed me a wink and fled before I could get another word in.

"Cheeky little shit," I murmured. Fi was always the one who could make me smile, no matter what. I turned my attention back to Glen. "So, what is it that's so important?"

"Just come with. It's in your apartment."

"About time you gave me back my key, bro."

"Yeah, yeah. What, you worried I'll bust in on you and whoever you've replaced me with?"

That was exactly my worry, but I wasn't going to say it to Glen. The guy was basically a straight shooter, so to speak, but I'd seen his jealous side when we were lovers, and it wasn't anything I had time for.

We got to my door and he knocked four times. I was about to point out that it was my place so I was fine to just go in, when an identical knock sounded from the inside.

"What the fuck, dude?"

HIS FATED MATE

"It's Alec."

I pulled out my key and unlocked the apartment. These two seemed to think they were secret agents all of a sudden.

When I pushed the door open, Alec stood in the entrance. He had his hands up, making a calm down motion. "Now, take it easy, Con."

"What the hell are you two up to?"

"Come on through."

"Giving me the grand tour? Can I just remind you I fucking live here? I know my way…"

My voice faded to nothing when I entered the living room and finally saw what these two knuckleheads had done. Bound to one of the kitchen chairs, with one of my old ties as a gag, was a Stoke Ridge man.

I didn't need the nose or the senses of

a wolf to tell that, either. It was all over him. The scents of the forest, and expensive soap, and good, rich living. Same as it was on every Ridgie, except it was much stronger on this one.

Because this one was Zoltan Valenta.

I turned to Glen first. "What the fuck is this, you idiots?"

"We found him creeping around in Bark Gully."

"Creeping?"

"Yep. Figured he was some kind of spy, probably come to sabotage the wedding."

I almost laughed at the idea of that. Alec and Glen obviously had no idea who they'd grabbed. Why would they? Neither of them had ever been to an official function in their lives.

"You guys realize I'm gonna get the blame for this. Don't you?"

HIS FATED MATE

"Blame?" Glen said. "Don't you mean *credit*? This'll get you back in the good books with your father."

"Wait... you haven't told anybody about this, have you?"

"Just a couple of the guys. We made sure to say it was all your idea. Y'know, so your dad—"

"Sure, whatever. Now listen, you two. Not a word about this to anyone else, okay?"

"Of course, Con."

"All right. We're done here, guys. Leave us."

"But we—"

"I said leave." It was a struggle to keep my voice—and my wolf—under control. It wasn't just my anger at what my guys had done here. It was also that heady mix of scents coming from Valenta.

EVIE RILEY

The guy was nothing like any man I'd ever been with. I had a type—or so I thought. Rough trade. Poor but hungry. Rugged, frayed around the edges, big enough to push back against me if I wanted them to.

Zoltan was the absolute opposite. Smooth and beautiful, his scent somehow both familiar and exotic at the same time. Even seated and bound, he had that regal bearing I remembered from years ago.

He was everything I believed I despised about pack leaders... and yet my heart was punching at me, and my belly was squirming. And my cock... holy fuck, my cock was as hard as hell.

Back when father still had me attending official functions, I'd seen this man—youth, back then—from across the room, or across the table, dozens of times.

HIS FATED MATE

I hadn't truly understood my own sexuality at the time, but he was the only part of those gatherings that I could remember with any clarity.

For all I knew, it was the sheer irresistible beauty of Zoltan Valenta that had confirmed my orientation for me.

I hadn't seen him in years, and I'd never been quite so close to him before. Now here he was, with his crisp sandy hair and his pale, unmarked skin, and I had to admit he'd always inspired feelings in me. And the feeling he mostly inspired was the desire to mess him the fuck up.

The guy had probably never done a lick of work in his life. Right here and now, as I stood over him, I suddenly had ideas for all kinds of work he could do for me.

And licking would definitely be a part

EVIE RILEY

of it.

CHAPTER FOUR

ZOLTAN

WHEN THOSE TWO oafs grabbed me in the forest, I almost capitulated and told them who I am. Whether they would have believed me, I'm unsure, but even if they did, it would have been almost impossible to explain why I'd been there.

Fate works in strange ways, though. All I'd wanted was to see, in person, the

EVIE RILEY

man who'd been terrorizing my troops, and now here he was. And of all people, it turned out to be the son of Patrick Blair.

He fit the description to a T. I had no doubt now that he was the troublemaker.

My senses told me he recognized me, too, so I'd felt sure that the moment he sent his underlings away, he'd release me. Still, he showed no sign of doing so. Just towered over me, with his thick arms crossed, and his steely eyes slicing through me. He hadn't even taken this damn gag off, yet.

He was everything I'd heard and imagined, and so much more. All except the part about being ugly as a bear. I couldn't imagine a single way the man could be any more attractive.

The years had been kind to Conall Blair; though perhaps it was a cruel type of kindness.

The handsome and intense young man had grown taller, broader, and more powerful. With his shoulder length hair as black as night, and the range of scars on his arms, and smaller marks on his face, he looked more like a pirate than the son of the Alpha.

Finally, he reached over and worked the tie out of my mouth and off over my head. Every move he made was definite. Abrupt, yet smooth, like flames dancing.

"You're early," he said.

"Excuse me?"

"Wedding's not for a couple days, yet. Are you that eager to get your paws on my sister?"

In the heat of Conall's aura I'd almost forgotten everything else in the world. I would say especially his sister, but it's impossible to forget someone you've never even seen.

He came around behind me and released the ropes securing my wrists. Then, he prowled back to the front of me. Even if I hadn't already known he was wolf, his fluid, predatory motion would have tipped me off.

When he knelt before me to untie my ankles, I barely contained my gasp of surprise. And it was at that moment I could finally admit to myself exactly why I had no interest in marrying this man's sister.

I'd never wanted anybody like I wanted Conall Blair. As frowned upon as it was in my pack, I couldn't deny the sweet tension in my core.

The howling of my wolf.

The blistering hardness of my cock.

"Oh, the wedding. No, that's not... um..."

Why was it so damn hard to think, or speak? I was the next in line to lead my pack. I'd been groomed from birth to handle... *situations*.

Yet, my heart beat against my ribs so hard I thought it might burst through.

The flash in Conall's eyes told me he sensed it, too, and my belly tightened in fear. I knew little of the ins and outs of Gray Vale, or their feelings about... *non-standard desires*, shall we say.

As he released the final knot, he showed concern on his gorgeous face for the first time. "You *are* planning to go ahead with the wedding?"

"I'm... confused, to be honest. I know what's riding on it, and I don't want to disappoint my father, or yours."

EVIE RILEY

"Believe me, buddy, Fiona's the one you don't want to disappoint. However shit-scared you are of your father, you should be doubly scared of my sister."

"Because that really makes me keen to go ahead with it."

A low growl sounded in Conall's throat, and my hackles stood up instinctively. Valenta men so rarely shifted. We had people to do that for us. But this man's intensity had my wolf pacing within me. Searching for a reason to come out.

Conall clearly sensed that turmoil instantly, as he gripped my shirt and hauled me up off the chair. Off my feet.

"You watch what you say about my sister, asshole."

Oh, holy hell. I was close to drowning in sensations. Not once in my life had I been threatened with anything more than sanctions, or the temporary denial of liberties. And only ever by my father.

No man or woman in Stoke Ridge would ever dare to treat me this way. Conall's aura grew bitter with threat and anger, and though I knew he could harm me as easily as breaking a twig, that couldn't divert the heady wash of desires pouring through me.

Still, that didn't mean I could simply push aside a lifetime of command training.

"It's not about your sister, Blair. Put me down."

"I'll fucking *knock* you down if you so much as breathe half a word against Fiona."

He dropped me to my feet, but kept a hold of my shirt. He never once turned the cold heat of his gaze away from me, though the hard ridge of his brow gradually softened.

His frown grew deeper again the moment he drew in a long breath. No doubt my own scents were telling him exactly what was running through my head.

"Wait," he said, his voice suddenly lower, and much darker. "You're telling me..."

I slid my hands up onto his wrists. "I'm saying I don't have any problem with your sister. At least, apart from the whole deal wherein she is, in fact, a woman."

"And you're... not into women?"

I tightened my grip, but struggled to find my voice. To say it out loud was such a big deal for a Stoke Ridge man. "I've never done anything. Never truly understood it until right now. But... as it turns out, no. I'm not."

"You're fucking kidding me." He tightened his mouth, and I couldn't help fearing I'd completely misjudged the situation, and the man.

Maybe Gray Vale was just as old-fashioned as my own pack. I probably shouldn't have relied simply on hearsay regarding Conall's sexuality. Especially hearsay from the men he bested in every fracas between the packs.

"You have a problem with that kind of thing, Blair?"

"With your sexuality? Not a single one." He shoved me back down into the chair, and turned on the spot, walking across the room shaking his head. "What I do have a problem with is you letting things get so far with this marriage."

"I never said I wanted it. But the needs

EVIE RILEY

of our packs dictate I still go ahead—"

He whirled and jabbed his finger toward me like he wished it was a spear. "You will do no such thing. My sister is not a toy to be... uh... toyed with."

Conall's eyes lit up, turning almost white with the heat of his twinned emotions. I could feel them as much as I could smell them. Anger weaving itself through arousal. His beast coursing through his blood, and pumping through his breath.

My own pulse quickened in reaction, my teeth tingling as they fantasized about becoming fangs. I sensed the sweet pain in Conall's mind as the same need pumped through him.

The room filled with the essence of this wild and beautiful man. My skin crackled with electricity, as his desire to shift reached out to my own wolf.

I'd heard fairytales in my childhood about this kind of thing. Wolves who were fated to be paired. But never had anybody said that it could happen between wolves of the same gender.

Was that just the old so-called morals coming through? Or was this, what was happening now between Conall and me... was this something completely new?

CHAPTER FIVE

CONALL

EVERYTHING I KNEW of this man, every way I'd ever experienced him, told me he was wrong for me. The beliefs he'd grown up with, the sheltered way he'd been raised, the sneering superiority that all Ridgies adopted when dealing with us.

Yet, I had to be honest to myself and say I'd never *actually* experienced this man. For a half dozen years, I'd glared across a table at him once every three months. Everything else I supposedly knew had come from second hand news, and my own assumptions.

Even now, as he stood with such lithe grace, and closed the distance between us, he was both everything I expected, and a complete surprise.

How could it be that he was hauling my wolf to the fore with nothing but his presence? He was locked up tight with the stupid pack peacemaking marriage situation that both our fathers still believed in. In other words, he was off limits to me in every fucking way.

Yet, the rich golden glow in his eyes drew me in, and made promises to every part of me. Both sides of me—man and wolf.

HIS FATED MATE

"So," Zoltan said, the soft music of his voice doing nothing to soothe my savage beast. If anything, it only made me wilder, and hungrier. "What happens now, big guy?"

"What happens now is that I take you…" I was trying to say I'd take him back home, but my wolf clamped around my throat before I could finish.

"Oh? Rather presumptuous, don't you think? Perhaps we could get dinner first."

There was that teasing little smile again, winding my brain into fuzz. My wolf had the fucking zoomies inside me, and it was all I could do to keep my human side in charge.

Zoltan's heat and scent clouded me, sending my breath into overdrive and short-circuiting my mind.

Finally, he let that delicious smile fade

EVIE RILEY

as he frowned with genuine concern. I couldn't imagine how I must look to him. Up close to him, my fists tight, my anger at my own confusion radiating like a physical force.

I thought at first he was scared. He wouldn't be the first man—or wolf—to react that way. But when he pressed his hand to the center of my chest, it was as if he'd hit me with a battering ram.

"Did you feel that?" he said, his voice low and ragged.

I clamped my hand over his and squeezed, searching for a path. A way out of this utter fucking mess. But all that skin to skin contact did was set off flares in my already smoldering head.

"Of course I felt it. I'd have to be dead not to."

Zoltan slid his hand free and moved it

higher, not stopping until he had his palm pressed to my cheek. Our faces were mere inches apart, a distance that was slowly but inevitably closing. I'm sure the sweet mix of confusion and hunger I saw in his eyes was reflected in my own.

"So, I guess I have to ask again," he murmured. "What happens now?"

In my whole life, I'd never been lost for words the way I was right then. So, I answered him the only way I could. By grasping his shirt and pulling him to me, taking his mouth in a kiss that seemed to transcend time and space.

I swore there were sparks literally flying from us as he opened for me, as I drove my tongue in to meet his. His soft moans played against my deep grunts, like a stream washing over rough rocks. Filling the gaps between them, slowly wearing them smooth.

I threw my arm around his taut, slender frame, gripping his firm ass and pulling him against me. The hard, raging heat of his cock ground against mine, and again the fireworks lit up inside my mind.

Though we'd only just officially met, and it defied any kind of rational explanation, Zoltan's body promised the kind of delights I'd sought, but never found, within the men of my own pack.

I slid my mouth down to his neck and bit into his flesh, hard enough to bruise him. But not nearly as hard as I wanted to. Wolves are hungry beasts.

Zoltan reached down between us, working at my jeans with an urgency that seemed almost life threatening.

The instant he got them open, a heavy pounding sounded on my apartment door, the noise hitting me like a fist made of cold water.

"Conall. You in there?"

Holy fuck. Of all the people it could have been.

"Uh… yes, father. Just a minute."

"Now, son. We have a shit storm brewing."

No prizes for guessing that particular shit storm involved my boneheaded buddies and my new boner-buddy.

I stepped backward and closed up my jeans again. There was no way I could risk speaking out loud to Zoltan, nor could I let father in to my room. He'd hear me, and no matter how well I hid the heir of Stoke Ridge, my father would scent him.

So, I put my finger to my lips, and hurried through to my closet, changing my shirt as quickly as I could. Whatever I could do to mask the heady aroma of this beautiful man.

"Son, come on."

"I'm here." I made a quick frowny face at Zoltan, who thankfully took the hint and scooted through to my bedroom. I took a half-second's pause as I pictured what I could get up to with him in there, and then slipped out of my apartment and into the line of fire.

"What's happening, father?"

"Can I come in?"

"No! Uh... it's a real mess in there. Fuckin' embarrassing, really. You'd think I'd grow up, huh?"

"It's my greatest hope, son. Then, if we can't go in, you'll walk with me." He marched off down the hallway and I followed along, feeling all of ten years old.

HIS FATED MATE

"Your future brother-in-law is missing. Anton Valenta is accusing us of foul play."

"That's, uh, a mighty big call. What's his proof?" Besides the man himself being in my apartment, of course.

"Nothing concrete, or we'd already be at war. But with all your recent antagonism along the border, can you blame them for thinking the worst of us?"

I began to protest my innocence when my father stopped short and silenced me with a big hand on my shoulder.

"Tell me you had nothing to do with Valenta's disappearance, son."

His *disappearance?* That was easy.

"I promise you, father. I had nothing to do with it."

"Good." He nodded as his grin grew predatory. "Then, we have the higher ground."

EVIE RILEY

"We do?"

"Oh, undoubtedly. We're not to blame."

"Wait. Have you asked anybody else?" My hackles rose, just from suddenly learning how my father saw me. That he believed I—and only I—would be reckless enough to interfere with the merging of the packs.

"Oh, you think I should ask Fiona? Has she ever struck you as impetuous?" He let out a quick, booming laugh. "Son, don't get your snout out of joint. You have a well known history. But now, it's his milksop son who's insulted *us* by fleeing."

How dare he insult Zoltan! My wolf growled so hard and deep inside me that the sound formed in my throat. I managed to cover it with a cough. How could I be so attached to the younger Valenta so quickly? To be so protective of his honor?

"Where do we go from here, father?"

"We're still formulating our strategy. But I need you confined to quarters for the time being." He clearly anticipated my reaction, holding up his hand for silence. And like I'd been trained to, I obeyed instantly.

"Son, this is your own doing. It's like the story of the boy who cried wolf, but in reverse. You're the boy who *was* wolf. You've bitten the Stoke Ridge pack too many times for them to allow you even the slightest benefit of the doubt."

I clenched my fists as my teeth tingled. Just because father was right, didn't make the bitter pill of truth any easier to swallow.

Still, being confined to quarters right now wasn't the punishment my father might believe it to be. I wouldn't be in solitary, after all.

CHAPTER SIX

ZOLTAN

I'D BEEN TRAINED in the art of patience all my life. Yet, waiting alone in Conall's apartment was a torture I was ill prepared to handle. To have had that brief taste of pure ecstasy, only to have it torn away just as quickly; to then sit idle and unaware, wondering at my fate... it would test any man.

EVIE RILEY

Of course, this heat I felt for Conall had to be nothing but a naïve infatuation. Something that took root before I was old enough to understand it, and which only grew over the years because in his absence, I'd cultivated an idealized version of him.

Now, it had become a flare. One that would burn too hot and brightly for either of us to handle, only to die out as quickly as it ignited.

That *had* to be the truth.

For the good of both packs.

So why did that flare feel more like a raging firestorm?

Why was my wolf suddenly prowling, and bristling, where he'd always been content to doze?

One way or another, I would be found and returned to Stoke Ridge. To the life I'd been born into, and the consequences of it. That was the way of things, and the way they should be.

But...

But what if that *wasn't* the way of things?

Or at least, not the *only* way?

For hours after being captured—right up until Conall appeared—I'd desperately hoped to be released and sent home. Suddenly, the instant the apartment door re-opened, I *dreaded* the idea that it was about to actually happen.

And then his scent came to me.

A moment later, Conall appeared in the doorway, as though my desire had pulled him all the way back.

"This is fucked up," he growled. "Seems everyone thinks I kidnapped you."

"Oh?"

EVIE RILEY

He let out a cold laugh. "Yeah. Apparently running around picking fights with people makes them think you're some kind of hothead."

"Hothead? I'd have said barbarian."

Conall smiled lightly as he ran his hands back through his thick hair and shook his head. He looked more of a lion than a wolf with that dark mane flying around him. My bones tingled as I studied him; the power in his movements, the confidence in his stance.

I was more like my own father than I cared to admit, most times. My power, my bearing—such as it might be—was entirely learned. *Cultivated.* I wore it like a ceremonial robe.

Conall's leadership qualities pulsed through his body, and glowed from his pores. The man simply owned any room, any space, he entered.

"So," he said, more of a growl than a word. "I'm under house arrest. Apparently father needs plausible deniability or some shit, and me running around out there isn't it."

"Does this count as irony, you think?"

"Yeah, maybe. But in any case, I can't go out there, and needless to say, neither can you, just yet." He sighed and leaned against the wall, all languid strength and graceful power. "You drink?"

"Not usually. I had plans to step up my game on my wedding night."

The exquisite torture of being so close to him, yet not touching him, became a physical pain. My wolf had always been well behaved, but he was truly flexing his power now. In ways I was entirely unprepared for.

EVIE RILEY

As Conall turned and headed toward his kitchen, I stood and followed along in his wake, though I'd had no conscious thought to do so. It was merely the feeling—the absolute certainty—that I needed to be exactly where he was.

My feet became independent, speeding me up until I was right behind him just as he reached the doorway. Conall spun instantaneously and reversed his momentum, slamming bodily into me and driving me back against the wall, as though he thought he was under attack. As though I had any ability to inflict the slightest pain on his impressive body.

I'd made no sound pursuing him, my inner beast exerting its influence on the outer me in ways I'd never experienced. His beast, on the other hand, was battle-hardened, and that was clearly one of the biggest differences between us.

"What the fuck are you doing, Valenta?"

"I honestly don't know. I'm... drawn to you."

"Well, fuckin' stop it." His heart punched at me through our chests, and mine punched back. Like neighbors complaining about the noise.

"I didn't start this, Conall. It has a momentum of its own."

His expression darkened as he tightened his grip on my shirt. "This can't happen, Zoltan."

"What can't?"

His broad shoulders swelled for a moment, as his wolf rearranged itself beneath his skin. His eyes flashed at me. It was probably meant to be a warning, but it felt so much more like a promise.

EVIE RILEY

"This."

He drove his mouth against mine, hard enough to slam my head back into the wall. I speared my hands into his hair and made fists, my every move governed by pure instinct. The same instinct that got me following him in the first place.

Conall's deep, sonorous voice filled my head and my heart and my lungs as he snarled out his base and brutal desires. He conquered my mouth, pure and simple, as he tore my shirt from my body.

His nails grew sharper as they thickened and lengthened, and he dragged them down my chest, drawing blood. Where I knew I should feel pain, I felt only release.

Bliss.

The big man hauled me up off my feet and swung around, slamming himself back against the wall without ever looking like breaking our kiss.

I threw my legs around him, climbing him like a tree and finding a level of brute strength within me that had never shown itself before. The harder I squeezed him, the deeper his growling voice fell.

He had the power to conquer me. Of that, there was no doubt. I was born to lead, yet was beyond ready to bow to Conall and his potent carnality.

I suckled on his thick tongue as he gripped my ass, pulling me against himself and grinding. Every way he touched me, in every place, burned like fire. We fell to the floor hard enough to break plain old human bones.

Only then did he take his mouth off mine, and only so he could bury his teeth into the flesh of my neck. I fisted his shirt and he let his wolf free just enough to swell his body and shred the fabric. The tattered garment came away in my hands as he dug his teeth into my chest, right where he'd already scratched me.

Conall swamped my nipple in his mouth and gripped my jeans, working them open in seconds. When he opened them and yanked down my underwear, my cock leapt free for a split second before his big, rough hand came down to capture it.

He made a fist so tight around me that I saw galaxies. I slammed my head back onto the floor as I arched my back. No hand had ever made me feel such blistering pleasure.

Not even my own.

With my hands still in his hair I clamped down, fisting that thick magnificence as he slid off my chest and headed south, stroking his hand up and down my length like he was starting an engine.

It took him an embarrassingly small amount of effort to shake himself loose of my grip and come up onto his knees, with one hand on the floor. As broad and attractive as his body was in a shirt, it was frighteningly magnificent bare. Scars peppered his arms and torso, beneath a neat coating of hair.

Still grinding my cock like he was beating a confession from it, he turned his face to the sky and arched his back, his breath coming in waves so thick they became sound. Grunts, moans, and the beginnings of howls.

Then, he dropped like he'd been shot, slamming his head into the center of my chest and I slapped my hands onto his shoulders, digging in my nails. Only when they pierced his skin did I realize I was as close to shifting as he was.

Conall swept down and pulled my whole cock into his mouth, down to the root. He made a tight fist around my balls as he pumped up and down, igniting fists of electricity up the length of my spine.

He yanked at my jeans and I writhed my way out of them, all without him releasing my cock from his mouth. When he reached up and jammed his finger into my mouth, I sucked like it was his cock until he dragged it back out.

Conall came up off me for a second, letting my cock slap against my belly. He growled out a *holy fuck* and then fell on me again, grinding his tongue up and down the length of me, then swamping my balls with the heaven of his mouth.

He gripped my ass and spread it, his wolf making deep snarling sounds in his throat. I grasped my knees and pulled, truly baring myself for the first time, and he drove his tongue against my rippled hole.

I finally knew exactly what had been missing from my few clumsy and abortive encounters with the women of my pack. It would have been the same problem even with the men there. No matter who I might have fucked from Stoke Ridge, I would *always* be the one in charge.

With Conall, that wasn't an option. His power was inseparable from his being, and at that moment I was his willing serf. I was in his thrall, and had been for far longer than I realized.

While he gripped my cock and stroked

it, he used his tongue to perfection. I simply opened to him, riding waves of bliss so unfamiliar to me, yet exactly what I'd always needed.

He replaced his tongue with his still wet finger, driving the tip inside me as he hauled my cock into his mouth again.

I threw my hands down and clawed at the carpet, shredding it as I fought the waves of pleasure buffeting my body. Conall had me so worked up I was teetering on the edge of a deep, narrow chasm. My wolf was on the other side, so close I could stroke him.

"Conall," I moaned, my throat tightening before I finished, drying up the sound. He snarled back at me, the sound more of a geyser, all heat and power. His wolf wrestled with his human side, his back rippling and his arms flexing. Still he hauled on my cock, the fiery heat of his mouth dealing the final blow to my resistance.

This magnificent man hunkered before me on all fours with his shoulders hunched. My fangs tingled as they grew, and the sensitive flesh of my cock told me his did, too. Our wolves met in the middle as I dived into the abyss.

My climax pierced me like a million silver bullets, and I filled Conall's mouth with my essence. He clamped around me, savoring every drop as his breath coursed across my belly.

When the waves of pleasure finally abated, he rose on his haunches, his form still human but his aura pure lupine.

He glared down at me, his wolf pacing just behind his glowing, ice blue eyes. Eyes I couldn't turn away from, revealing

EVIE RILEY

a soul I couldn't resist.

CHAPTER SEVEN

CONALL

ALL MY LIFE, I'd felt alive. It sounds obvious, of course. But I had *never* felt as complete, as entirely *vital*, as I did at that moment. The heat of Zoltan's fluid still in my mouth, the rich musky flavor of him existing more as a concept even than as a reality.

My own wolf roared at me to take what

EVIE RILEY

I was owed. What I'd earned. Well, it was either my wolf or my balls, and not for the first time I couldn't separate one from the other.

Whichever part of me it was, the rest my body obeyed instinctively. No need for any interference from my mind.

I grasped Zoltan by the legs and flipped him onto his belly, diving down to swathe the crease of his ass with my tongue, still coated in his juice.

He arched his back and moaned, propping himself up to me. I let his come gush from my mouth as I worked my tongue inside him, and it was the perfect blend of my two halves. Human and beast working hand in paw.

Harder and deeper I stroked and prodded him with my come-covered tongue, getting him all greased up and ready. My wolf was impatient at the best of times. And this moment was absolutely the best of times, so his lupine patience was absolutely nonexistent.

"Please, Conall..." Zoltan's need was a physical presence in the room.

I pumped two fingers deep into him as I came up on my knees. In seconds, I had my jeans open and my cock practically cheered.

"You have a fuckin' beautiful ass, man."

Before he could reply, I fisted my cock and nudged it in place. I had to keep reminding myself this was his first time. The guy was just so fucking into it he seemed like a veteran.

I sank my half-claw nails into his hips, drawing blood, as I punched my cock forward.

EVIE RILEY

Zoltan hissed as he stretched around me, but he bounced forward and back to get me deeper inside as quickly as possible.

Shifters run hotter than regular humans, and that was never more obvious than when I had my cock buried inside one. But nobody had ever burned into me the way Zoltan did. It went beyond pure heat, expanding into the crackling of electricity, the viscous bubbling of lava.

"Oh, fuck... Conall..."

I took his sandy hair in my fist and dragged on it, pulling him up until his hands left the floor. Yanking backward in harmony with every forward punch of my hips, admiring the ballet of his body as it reverberated with the hard impacts.

His creamy skin glowed under the

coating of sweat I'd put there. His taut muscles danced along with the writhing of his wolf, until it wasn't clear which side of him I was watching.

I'd been a player for more years than I'd care to admit. Always searching for more than I found, forever hungry for deeper connection.

Turns out, all along I'd been searching for exactly what I'd found here. A man equal but different, whose strengths bolstered my weaknesses, whose needs embraced my gifts.

And whose ass was as tight as a fucking vise.

I sat back on my haunches, dragging him with me. Zoltan slammed back against my body, his skin gliding across my chest as sweat met sweat. The delicious savory scents of his sweat, his cock, his armpits, his every fucking pore, filled my nose and my head and my heart.

Every harsh, driving pump of my hips, he let out a sweet, whining moan, and slammed himself down on my length, working me just as hard as I worked him.

"Fuck me, Zee... I'm going..." Forming the words was the hardest thing I'd ever done. My jaw was the wrong shape, already narrowing and stretching as every muscle and bone in my body twitched, anticipating a shift.

My wolf hunkered down, feet spread, and took a deep breath. I closed my eyes, and threw my arms around Zoltan's body, bending him forward as I clamped my teeth into the flesh of his neck.

And as my climax erupted, my beast arched, taking me with it. I curled back on myself, dragging Zoltan with me, every hot, frenzied jet of fluid from my cock accompanied by a howl from the beast inside me, and a gush of blood across my tongue.

My muscles rolled and rippled, my bones shuddered, as I pumped my climax deep into this beautiful man. The world flashed perfect ice blue behind my closed eyes, pulsing in rhythm with my cock.

Time meant nothing. We stayed there, locked together, for as long as it took. Two men and two wolves, somehow becoming a single entity for a window of time.

All the stories I'd ever heard about fated mates had been like fairytales. Even to the point they'd only ever described it happening between males and females.

Suddenly, here we were. This was the final confirmation for me, of all my suspicions. Never had I experienced a totality like the one that still had me wrapped up in its warmth.

A fated mate, who was a fucking Stoke Ridge man. All my life I'd ruled them out as anything but snobbish and soft, and now I was fucking lost inside one. Metaphorically as well as physically.

After who knows how long, I eased my teeth out of his delicious flesh, and Zoltan raised himself off me. My eyes spun as I searched for a way back into the real world.

My lover fell forward, landing on the floor of the hallway in complete exhaustion. Blackness swelled inside my head, and it took all my effort to control my own descent.

I landed on Zoltan's back and slid to the floor, one arm and one leg tossed over his body in possession. His invigorating scent was the last thing I comprehended before I lost myself to the darkness.

CHAPTER EIGHT

ZOLTAN

I RARELY DREAM. Or at least, I barely ever remember anything by the time I wake. This time, I absolutely inhabited my dream world, because I was not alone. I had Conall with me. A bristling black wolf with eyes of perfect ice blue.

Time had no meaning as we ran together, and wrestled, and play-hunted.

EVIE RILEY

He kept leaping over objects—boulders, fallen trees—and disappearing for minutes at a time. Whenever he did, my whole body went cold, and the entire world was a dark abyss. Only when he came back out of hiding did the color and light return.

After a time, I realized I wasn't entirely dreaming. That I was partway between sleeping and waking, and that Conall himself was leaving me where I lay, for minutes at a time, only to come back and wrap himself around me.

All I wanted right then was for him to roll me down onto my back and make love to me again.

Wait a minute.

Make love?

Could we even call it that?

When it was so carnal, so impetuous.

HIS FATED MATE

So... *lupine.*

A heavy pounding noise hauled me all the way up to full consciousness. For the briefest instant, I luxuriated in the heat of Conall's body, curled around mine once more. I brushed my fingers over the sweet ache on my neck, where he'd marked me.

Made me his own.

The pounding at his door sounded again, and we both sprang to a crouching position. Wolf instincts always came through in a crisis.

The booming voice of Patrick Blair came through the closed door. "Son, you'd better be in there. If I find out you're sniping at those fucking Ridgies again..."

Conall let a low growl rumble in his chest, and I felt his fear and anger as if they were my own. The power of his bite at work.

EVIE RILEY

He shot me a fierce look, though it didn't take any sensing between us for me to understand what was at stake here. It didn't matter how things *were*, it only mattered how things *looked*. And this made Conall look guilty as hell.

Together we stood, prowling silently away from his front door. He led me through to the back of his apartment, and the small balcony that came off his spare bedroom. We were still naked, we were thirty feet up, and there was nothing but wide fields behind the building.

In any case, we were out of options. Conall pulled me to him and planted a deep, lingering kiss on my lips that had a real tang of regret to it. Then, he climbed over the railing and swung himself down to the balcony below.

It took me a few seconds to get my

brain working again after that kiss. I wasn't sure I had the agility to follow Conall, but my decision was again made for me when the front door of the apartment burst open.

"Conall! Son, don't you fucking test me."

I clambered over the railing and hung down from the edge. Conall grabbed my legs and pulled me to safety beside him.

"Gonna have to jump from here, Zee."

"It's twenty feet."

"Then let's do it the easy way," he murmured.

"Easy way? What do you mean?"

He shot me a lighting fast wink. "Do you even shift, bro?"

"Um... no, not really."

His surprise flashed on his face for a moment. "Might be time to refresh your memory, then."

He crouched and let his shift take over. In seconds, he was wolf, and exactly as he'd appeared in my dream. Fur as black as midnight with eyes like glowing ice. He did it so easily, so naturally. Like he was changing a shirt.

He licked my leg, urging me again to shift as well. It was my only option, but I was so out of practice. Only by once again grinding my fingertips into the sweet bruise on my neck did I gain the confidence I needed.

I dropped to my knees and closed my eyes, letting my wolf free—*truly free*—for the first time. Every other time I'd shifted had been for ceremonial reasons.

The sharp-winged butterflies in my belly flew through my limbs, cutting away everything human and leaving only wolf behind in their wake. The world became uncomfortably bright and impossibly fragrant.

There was no time to savor the moment. Patrick Blair's swearing from the floor above got me raising my hackles, and the instant Conall leapt over the balcony and dropped the two stories to the ground, I once again followed him.

Together, we fled across the fields, heading for the distant forested hills. The world hit me like a slap in the face, and I realized I'd never been wolf out here. Out in nature, where it really mattered. I'd only ever shifted in halls and rooms.

My body pulsed with energy as I ran and leapt, and I couldn't keep my head still. The wash of scents poured into me until I overflowed with sensations. I had no idea where we were headed, but all I knew was I had to follow my mate.

Holy hell that sounded weird.

My mate.

I knew it beyond any doubt, though. Conall was mine and I was his. The ideas and the concepts were too hard to fathom with wolf thoughts, but the truth was so basic and perfect it needed nothing but instinct to understand it.

As we ran, I sensed the utter joy radiating off Conall's wolf as well, though it was tinged with something else. Something murky and vague, reminiscent of that tinge in his kiss just before. All I could tell was that, again, I'd need my human side to understand it. But it was such a weak trace that I doubted my human would detect it.

We ran on, chasing after rabbits and birds, with no real intent. The thrill came from the pursuit, from the rush of fear we instilled. From impacting on the world around us, even in only a tiny way.

This wasn't leadership. This wasn't the destiny I was born to. This was pure, wonderful freedom. And I could get used to it so easily.

Only when we'd gone deep into the forested hills did we come to a halt. We stopped at a stream and jumped in, the icy water as sharp and refreshing as Conall's bite was only hours before.

When my mate shifted back, I followed along. The process was so much easier already.

He climbed out and sat on a flat rock, dangling his feet in the water, and I swam over to him, standing on the bed of the stream, my body between his knees, my face level with his thick chest.

EVIE RILEY

Conall cupped my head in his palm and I leaned into his touch. All I could scent on him now was the joy from earlier. Anything else had been washed off in the water.

But even as he bent to kiss me, his eyes held a sadness I couldn't yet read. He was still too new to me.

The touch of his lips to mine eased my worries instantly. Even in the cold water, this man had me hotter than hell. I opened to him, dancing my tongue around his as he gripped my hair and claimed my mouth.

I knew then that this man was my food, my drink, my soul. There was no longer any reason for me to return to Stoke Ridge. Maybe we couldn't stay here in Gray Vale, but my place was beside Conall, for eternity.

HIS FATED MATE

He snarled and broke our kiss, pushing me back far enough to glare down into my eyes. I could almost see words dancing behind his lips, though I couldn't read their intent.

"Zee, please..." That was all he said before I had my fist around his cock, and his balls in my other hand.

"You have nice manners for a barbarian," I murmured. And that was all I said before I drove my mouth down the length of his incredible cock.

CHAPTER NINE

CONALL

NO. HE HAD to stop.

Oh, fuck...

Zoltan had me deep in his mouth, and the sensation went so far beyond pleasure it was almost unrecognizable. He'd been working me for under a minute and I was close to finishing already.

I never should have given him my

mark. That was fucking stupid, but I'd had no control of myself at that moment. He'd spoken to a deep part of me that I'd never explored, in either form.

But this definitely *had* to stop. I'd already made too many mistakes, and this was one I couldn't let continue. This had to be the line I drew in the sand.

For too long, I'd enjoyed my privilege without taking the responsibilities that went with it. As difficult as it was, I had to put my own wants—needs—last this time. The packs needed this man to marry my sister.

"Please, Zee... you gotta... oh, fuck..."

He climbed out of the stream and slammed his hand into my chest, knocking me flat on my back. He never once let my cock slip from his mouth as he prowled up beside me, spinning around so we could both fit on the rock.

My climax simmered just below boiling point, but I couldn't just let things go on like this. If he wouldn't end it, then I had to.

But that line I drew just a moment ago... I wasn't so much toeing it as struggling not to leap across it.

Until finally, I let out a long moan that became a ragged snarl, and gripped Zoltan's leg. I rolled onto my side and pulled him over to me, hauling his cock down my throat.

Again, my mark was a blessing and a curse. Every stroke of his mouth down my length, and my mouth down his, only bound us tighter. And the tighter our bond, the harder the impact, the farther the fragments would fly, when I had to break it.

EVIE RILEY

But holy fuck. This moment was sheer perfection, as his body completed mine.

I gripped his thighs and dragged him closer to me, driving my own hips toward his beautiful face until there was nothing between us but sweat and water.

My climax hovered, closer than ever, and Zoltan's kept pace. We circled each other, connected in every way that mattered.

My spine fizzed as it buckled, stretching and thickening as my wolf flexed his muscles. Zoltan's strength grew as he plunged his length deep into my throat, and we rolled as we wrestled.

The bliss when my climax hit was matched only by the musky heat of Zoltan bursting in my mouth at the exact same instant. We formed a complete circle, each drinking the other's essence as we buried our half-shifted claws into the flesh we desired so much.

Still, we rolled, until we came free of the rock and plunged into the icy water again. Only then did we separate, each of us finding his way to the surface through the now fading red mist of arousal.

I clambered up onto the bank on one side of the stream. Zoltan ended up on the other, and though my mate couldn't realize it, it was the perfect sign for what was about to happen.

A sign that made itself clear an instant later, when heavy footsteps came thudding through the brush on the far side of the stream. No Gray Vale man would make such a fucking noise, so I knew exactly what was about to happen.

Zoltan fired a worried look at me, and I looked away in shame. His puzzlement pulsed through my veins and my anger at myself grew beyond belief. When Zoltan pressed his fingers to the mark on his shoulder, we both groaned in pleasurable pain. And it was clear just how strong our bond was.

A figure stepped out from behind a tree, on Zoltan's side of the stream. A man wearing the patrol uniform of a Ridgie. Exactly as I'd asked for when I contacted Anton Valenta while Zee slept in my hallway.

The patrolman stopped short the moment he saw us, a puzzled expression on his face. "What the hell is happening here?"

Typical Ridgie reaction to nudity, as always. I shook my head as I stood. "Man, we had to shift to get away. You guys really need to lighten up."

HIS FATED MATE

I finally summoned up the guts to look at Zoltan again. And I instantly regretted it. The pain of betrayal was written all over him. "You... called them? You planned this?"

"*Planned* is way too fancy a word. I took the only available moment, and did what had to be done." I took a ragged breath and fought down the red hot waves of loathing I had for myself. "It's time I stepped up. For the future."

"What the hell are you talking about? This is not stepping up. It's turning tail."

"You have a prior commitment, Zee." I barely whispered it, yet I knew he heard.

"But what about..." His throat tightened, and our bond told me it was a toxic cocktail of hopes smashed and beliefs betrayed.

This was the future of longing and

torture I'd made for us both. I'd marked him, made him my own, and no matter where he was and who he was with, I'd feel him.

And he'd feel me.

He stood abruptly, glaring across the divide between us. "I thought we'd—"

"Remember where you are, Zee," I murmured. The return of the heir would be a most welcome event for the Ridgies. I doubted they'd celebrate the combination of coming back and coming out.

He growled out his anger. "I know where I am. More importantly, I know where I *should be*, Con." He took the shirt his patrolman offered, and tied it around his waist. His voice turned soft and smooth, almost boyish. "Tell me honestly this is what you truly want. Make me believe it really is for the best."

HIS FATED MATE

There was no way I could do that. I'd made a habit over the years of lying to lovers, with the express goal of making them ex-lovers. But even if I wanted to lie now, it simply wasn't possible.

I rubbed my fingers over my own neck, in exactly the place where my mark was on Zoltan.

"I had to do it, Zee. It was for the good... of the packs." My chest tightened so hard I could barely breathe, let alone speak. The pain of the moment was so great, I might as well be cutting my own leg off. The difference being that I could still live without my leg.

Zoltan spoke no more. He just turned and walked out of my sight.

Out of my life.

CHAPTER TEN

ZOLTAN

IT WAS MY wedding day, and I was nothing but a shell. I'd dodged the barrage of questions when I arrived home, and had barricaded myself away to let my soul bleed out.

Since Conall cut my heart to ribbons, I'd barely spoken at all. Not even to my father, though I couldn't be sure whether he noticed. At this point, I was little more than a chess piece to him, in any case.

Worst of all, my wolf paced and howled and nipped at my conscience. I should probably call the ASPCA on myself, the way I'd neglected him since my return.

He—*I*—could still sense everything about Conall. Not as a memory, not as a dream, but as a part of my own mind and body, in the here and now.

His ongoing irritability coursed through my blood, though it carried resounding echoes of rage.

There was no way to reconcile his betrayal with his current state of mind. His anger stemmed from hunger. Hunger for me, even though he'd deceived and dismissed me as effortlessly as he'd seduced me.

Why the hell had he given me his mark

if he'd never intended to keep me?

I was in limbo, though it felt more like purgatory.

This impending marriage had already been on shaky ground, and now Conall had completely doomed it. I could never be anyone else's mate but his. It was the same for him. That was the nature of the mark. Nothing but death could end the bond.

Yet, here I was, minutes away from marrying his sister.

How could I even look at my bride without picturing her brother?

Worse still, how could I ever make whole our union when I clearly had no sexual interest in her entire gender?

After all, the purpose of these marriages was to give the packs a common heir. To unite our people, for peace. So folks had always said, especially my father over the past few months.

There was no way that was ever happening. Not between Fiona and me, at least. She'd have to hire in a stunt double to put a bun in *her* oven. Without my mate, I honestly believed I would never get hard again.

Of course, every time I closed my eyes and opened my heart, Conall came rushing back in and proved that belief entirely wrong. Though I strove to hate the man, just the sense of him was enough to get me hard.

What good was a hard cock, though, when your mate was off limits?

What good was *anything*?

Father pounded on the door, breaking through my near catatonia. All that did was take me straight back to the stolen night in Conall's apartment. The morning that was torn apart by *his* father knocking. And though I didn't know at the time, by my lover's deception.

"Son? It's starting."

I winced and shook my head, searching for a way out of this mess. But I'm a man of duty; born into it, and bred to embrace it.

There was no room anymore for me to question my place. I'd long ago accepted exactly which cog I was in the big machine. For what felt like a single heartbeat, I'd outrun it. That brief window of time with Conall, where I'd experienced pure joy and belonging, was over.

Dead.

The problem was, he'd be my brother-in-law. I couldn't put him out of my mind, or out of my life. He was up there, right now. Not just in the congregation, but right up in my face. An integral member of the wedding party.

As an only child, and the Alpha in waiting, I'd had nobody to act as the equivalent of a best man. So, of course, my father organized a suitable stand-in. The only man with the status befitting such an honor.

Conall *fucking* Blair.

How the hell would I get through this without confessing my feelings for him, either accidentally or willingly, through words or actions?

That was the real trouble. My hatred for what he did could barely surface through my desire for who he truly was. I already knew him as well as I knew myself. It was impossible not to, thanks to his fucking mark.

"Son? If you've disappeared again—"

"I'm here, father."

"Well? Don't keep the packs waiting."

I opened the door and father blessed me with the only genuine smile I could remember seeing from him in months.

Maybe even years.

"Son, I'd begun to think this day would never come."

"Yes, father."

He softened visually. "I'm sorry I rode you so hard, son. You're doing the right thing, though. You know how the tradition works."

I sure did. As if I hadn't felt enough pressure already. With no surviving brothers, I was the only one who could be the next unopposed Alpha of Stoke Ridge. And the only one who could then supply a

EVIE RILEY

Valenta heir.

Should I step aside, it would mean anybody could challenge for pack leadership. So, in addition to being railroaded into marrying someone other than my fated mate, I also had twenty generations sitting on my shoulders.

"Come on, son. Time to take your place in history."

This was it. I was to pledge my life to someone I didn't, and couldn't, love. Three days ago, I was fully prepared to accept that as my lot in life. How quickly everything changed.

I simply had to put Conall out of my mind.

The moment I walked into the hall, it was clear to me that *I* was the one who was out of my mind. To ever think I could suppress my feelings for Conall Blair.

HIS FATED MATE

With father beside me, I trudged up to the altar, missing my mother more than I had in many a year.

My body tensed before my mind even gave the order. I'd believed I could handle this moment. I was wrong.

My mate stood in place, looking somehow as if he could simultaneously host an award ceremony, and commandeer a scurvy crew of buccaneers. And searing my damn soul with those crystalline eyes.

My mark pulsed, heavy with his emotions. Those emotions manifested words in my head. Disbelief that I was still going through with the wedding. Shame at his own actions.

And desire.

Pure, ravenous and scorching.

The sheer power of his hunger had my

knees buckling and my wolf bristling. Even my father, standing the other side, sensed a change in me, and put his hand around my arm, holding me up.

"What is it *now*, son?"

The blend of distaste and disapproval in his tone was exactly what I needed to get through this. His cold disappointment was the perfect shield for Conall's lust.

"Nothing, father. I'm just soaking up the gravity of the moment."

"Well, do it privately. Show no weakness. You're the next Alpha. Of both packs."

"What?" This wedding was supposed to settle the petty arguments between packs. Join them in spirit, not in law. In short, it was meant to be a marriage, not a coup. "What have you put in place, father?"

"Don't concern yourself, son. Just

stand there and marry that... *woman.*"

It didn't take a lot of imagination to realize he'd said *woman*, but meant a whole other five-letter word. One that was even worse for wolves than for humans, since it leveled totally different insults at both halves.

Bitch.

Music began, and the bride-to-be appeared at the end of the aisle, with her father. Though she was dressed in a white strapless dress, at least she'd managed to eschew the wearing of a veil.

Fiona Blair shared her brother's intense beauty, though her features were of course much finer and more delicate. The lack of scarring on her face and shoulders suggested she didn't share her brother's reckless nature, at least.

They came toward me, but though I

watched them, my entire focus was off to the side. I swore I was getting a sunburn from the heat of Conall's glare.

Patrick Blair released his daughter's arm, and she let out a small sigh that sounded for all the world like resignation.

I was supposed to do something at that point, but my mind was a sizzling pan, and every thought bit into me like spitting oil.

Fiona stepped right up beside me, then reached over and took her brother's hand with a smile.

Conall pulled her to him and the siblings shared a tight hug. I couldn't help but envy their closeness, and it reawoke my sadness at losing my mother and unborn brother when I was so young.

Over his sister's shoulder, Conall speared me again on those hard but heavenly eyes of his. My mark pulsed harder than ever and I gasped with the ecstatic agony of it.

And between us, the slender figure of Fiona jolted. She pushed out of her brother's embrace and held him at arm's length.

He dragged his steely gaze away from me and met his sister's eyes. Not a word passed between them, but she tilted her head, raising it as though scenting prey.

Slowly, she turned toward me, a frown creasing her forehead.

When the celebrant began speaking, Fiona held up her hand to silence him. She stepped up closer to me, drawing in a deep breath.

"What the hell is going on?" my father growled. "You damn Valentas are making a mockery of—"

EVIE RILEY

"Quiet!" Fiona's voice sliced through the moment, and for the first time I'd ever known, my father—the Alpha of Stoke Ridge—was silenced.

My bride-to-be took my hands in hers, and looked me over, from head to toe and back again. "Oh, this is too bad. You're absolutely lovely."

"I, uh..."

"Where is it?"

"W–what do you mean?"

"His mark."

What the hell? How did she know?

I glared at Conall. "You told her?"

Conall shook his head, but never even looked like breaking eye contact.

"He didn't have to, Zoltan," Fiona murmured. "I have a gift. Dubious as it might be." This last part she said over her shoulder, and it was clearly directed to her twin brother.

"Sis—"

"You shut up, too, Con."

Fiona turned and addressed the congregation. "I'm sorry, everyone. I'm afraid the wedding is off."

Fiona walked back down the aisle, her head still held high, her gait easy and relaxed, as if she did this kind of thing every day.

And though I took comfort that, for the moment, all eyes were on her, I knew it wouldn't last. The instant she walked out of here, it would be my head on the chopping block.

CHAPTER ELEVEN

CONALL

LIKE EVERYBODY ELSE, I simply watched in awe as Fiona sauntered back out, apparently unruffled by what she'd just learned about her ex-fiancé and me.

Despite the fact I knew her better than anyone, I couldn't be certain she wasn't in pain. That she didn't hate me.

Not to mention Zoltan would be right

in the firing line here, and despite everything I'd done, every mistake I'd made, and every barrier I'd put between us... he was my mate. He, more than anyone, was my responsibility here. To protect, and to nurture. And the only way I could do that would be to get him the fuck away from this farce.

I leaned over and murmured to him to follow me, and though he pulled away like I'd cut him, he did as I asked.

My father blocked our path for a moment. "Son, what the hell happened?"

"I promise I'll tell you, just as soon as we have a handle on it, father. Right now, we need to check on Fiona."

I definitely knew father well enough to manipulate him. As patriarchal and condescending as it was, he'd always been overprotective of Fiona. She was his biggest blind spot, and his greatest weakness. If only he could recognize she was truly his greatest asset.

Zoltan followed me out of the hall and around the corner, where we found Fiona gazing out over the scenery. The hills and mountains of Stoke Ridge and out to the plains and valleys of Gray Vale.

"Fi," I said. "Talk to me."

She whirled on the spot, jabbing me right in the chest. "Why the hell didn't you tell me?"

"Fi, this wasn't something we planned. It was... fuck, it was about as far from planned as anything could be."

"No excuse, bro. You were going to let this go ahead, anyway? And you?" She turned her irritation to Zoltan. "How exactly did you think this was going to work between us, when we already have

EVIE RILEY

this asshole between us?" She indicated me with a casual toss of her thumb over her shoulder.

Zoltan's beautiful features hardened, and he turned to me while speaking to Fiona.

"Because that asshole betrayed me and tossed me aside."

"That's not what I did," I muttered, though of course it was *exactly* what I did. "You know why I had to send you home, Zee."

He laughed, a cold, hard burst of sound, and spread his arms to encompass the whole situation around us. "For this? You shouldn't have. You *really* shouldn't have."

It didn't matter he was exactly right. It didn't matter that I'd absolutely fucked things up, and maybe risked my relationship with my sister along with it.

I'd fought battles against man and beast, any one of which could have ended me. Never once had I panicked or lost my head.

As much as I tried to tell myself I'd been working for the greater good, I knew in my heart I'd been nothing more than a scared little boy.

The threat of death had never paralyzed me. No, it took the threat of love to do that. Pure, shameful panic in the face of my own stupid fucking feelings.

That was why I'd called Anton Valenta. That was why I betrayed all that mattered to me.

Now, all that mattered to me was undoing the damage. Earning my mate back.

Fiona reached out to us both, one

hand on my shoulder, one on Zoltan's. "You boys will be the death of me. And of our packs."

"Zee," I said. "I know it can't erase anything, but I'm so fucking sorry. It was pure cowardice on my part to send you home."

"That part was your duty, Conall," he replied. "I could accept that—maybe even respect it—if that was what really drove your actions. What hurt was that you hid your intentions. That you lied straight to my face."

He tore open his shirt, pointing at my mark, and my wolf hunkered down, hungrier than ever for this man, and ready to pounce. "Your cowardice was in giving me this, with no thought to the ramifications."

"For fuck's sake, you two." Fiona

landed a light slap on each of our cheeks. "This is why our packs are damned. We've been led by men for too long without any balance."

Zoltan straightened his back as if he'd been personally insulted. "Tradition dictates—"

"Screw tradition," my sister countered. "You boys have such a warped sense of duty, and no understanding of self-sacrifice."

"Sis, how can you say that? I gave up my life's happiness so this wedding could go ahead."

"Yes. That's exactly the problem. It's what I've tried to tell you basically forever, bro. Men don't self-sacrifice right. For you guys, it's always a blaze of glory, all or nothing, liberty-or-death kind of situation. Either through nature or nurture, we women self-sacrifice daily. We step around an obstacle, rather than blasting it apart. We take the small hits so nobody has to jump on a damn grenade. Metaphorically speaking."

I couldn't tell if she was right in a global sense. But holy fuck, she was absolutely right about me. My behavior compared to hers.

Zoltan chuckled at my obvious discomfort, but Fiona thudded the heel of her hand into his chest. "You don't get off lightly here, mister. I was prepared to take my lumps and marry you, sight unseen, because it was for the greater good. But that was when I believed it would be a... well, let's say a *fruitful* marriage."

"I apologize, Fiona. But as the daughter of the Alpha, you must understand the pressures on me, to some degree."

"The pressures, yes. Your actions, no. You're still a man, capable of independent thought and decision. Were you *ever* planning to tell me you're gay?"

"Gay? He's not *gay*." The booming voice of Anton Valenta sounded behind me, where he and my father had come to check on us. "While I hear that kind of sin is all the rage in Gray Vale, it simply doesn't happen in higher packs like Stoke Ridge."

I made fists as I turned to face the man. "The only way your pack is higher than mine is simple geography."

Anton raised one eyebrow. "The savage speaks." He glanced at my hands and rolled his eyes. "And I see you're already regressing to your barbarous ways. You are aware that you'd be excommunicated for striking an Alpha, boy?"

"Conall," my father said. "Stand down."

The punishment would just about be worth it. The seams of my tux whined in pain as my wolf asserted himself. I spread my feet as the shift threatened to take over me.

"Oh, put it away, son," Anton said, sneering at me.

"Not your son," I growled.

"Fi?" father said.

"Enough."

Fiona's tone was all business, and sliced through the moment effortlessly. She even managed to get my wolf to stand down.

"Look at you all," she continued. "Con, I love you to death, bro, but you need to calm the fuck down. There's a wide and bountiful middle ground between wolf and human, but you only ever leap from one side to the other. And you—"

She stabbed the air in front of Anton Valenta's face. Where my rage had only made him annoyed, her disappointment had him flinching.

"Don't you have more important things to do than baiting my brother?"

"I was planning to preside over this wedding, but clearly you have cold feet now, girl. Why else would you make such fanciful claims about my son."

My wolf snarled again, as he always did whenever someone spoke against my sister.

And once again, she cut through the moment. "Conall. Get your shit together, bro." Her strong tone worked on me so much better than shouting would.

Anton continued, as though oblivious

to my wolf and the threat it posed. "It's of no concern, in the end. I never thought you worthy to be elevated to Stoke Ridge."

The honor of my pack, of my family, of my sister, had been called into question once too often. My wolf could simply take no more. He sank his teeth into my mind, and I fell into a crouch to let the shift take over.

CHAPTER TWELVE

ZOLTAN

I WAS STILL in awe of the way Fiona Blair simply took control of the situation. As much as it could be controlled, anyway, with Conall ready to shift at the drop of an insult.

When it was clear my mate had succumbed to his basest instincts, I felt a burst of heat in my chest, and a charge of panic in my mind.

My mark burned and jolted, like it was going to leap free of my body.

"Zoltan?" Fiona said. "Your move."

"What?"

"He's only going to respond to you, now. Step up, buddy."

Conall grunted as if in pain, resisting the shift his wolf demanded. His agony called me through our bond, through his mark, and everything became clear to me in an instant.

His sister was right. Only *I* could reach him now, and break through his rage. And the consequences of failure could be fatal. Perhaps even cause a proper pack war.

But to soothe my mate now would mean admitting my relationship with him. I'd be confessing my orientation—my so-called *sins*—to my father. Coming out, when I'd barely even come to realize I'd been *in*.

In the end, that was a small price to pay. Either he'd accept me as I am, or I'd be the one excommunicated. Whichever way it went, there was one thing I knew about myself, and it was that I was never meant to be Alpha. I would rather be happy than in command, and for me, the two were mutually exclusive.

And despite everything, the only way I could be happy was with this man before me. I needed him the way he needed me. The way we both needed water and food.

I crouched before Conall's tortured form, and pressed my palm to his fevered cheek. He jerked his head up and glared deep into me, his eyes burning like sunlight on snow.

EVIE RILEY

My mate's features contorted as his wolf flexed beneath the surface.

"Conall," I murmured, barely more than a whisper. "Breathe for me. Slowly."

He gripped my forearm, sinking his half-formed claws through my skin. I hissed with pleasure as much as with pain, and slid my hand down to his neck.

He mirrored me, pressing his other hand onto my neck and finding his mark. The instant he made contact, it was as if we'd completed a circuit, and his anger flowed into me. My wolf jolted, hackles rising, but as always, a burden shared is a burden halved.

With the two of us riding the wave of rage, quelling it became so much simpler. It was another blessing—and sometimes curse—of the mate bond.

Gradually, his claws retracted, and the

heat of his rage cooled. Finally, we were both back under control of our human sides, and we stood.

Unfortunately, the skin to skin contact had other consequences. Big, hard ones, which were obvious to all around us.

"Zoltan?" my father said, through clenched teeth. "What the hell is going on here? This was to be the culmination of years of work."

"I thought it was to be my wedding, father."

"Let's not split hairs." He shot his harsh Alpha glare at the Blair pack. First Patrick, then Fiona, neither of whom flinched.

Before he turned his rage on Conall, I slipped my hand into my mate's grip. Letting him know I was there for him. Hoping to convey with just a touch that I

EVIE RILEY

understood what he'd tried to do—for me as well as himself—and that I could even forgive him. And to encourage him to keep his wolf tethered. At least until we could get some time together.

Father's searing gaze threatened to slice right through both of us. The instant he saw our hands clasped, his own wolf seemed to awaken.

"Zoltan? What is the meaning of this?"

I raised my hand, bringing Conall's along for the ride.

"Yes, well... about that, father. I'm sorry you had to find out this way."

"Find out? Zoltan, this... thing you think is happening? It's a lie. No Alpha of Stoke Ridge has ever had this kind of... perversion. More to the point, no son of mine would even entertain the possibility."

HIS FATED MATE

"Perhaps I'm adopted."

The growl that burst from father's throat was three-quarters wolf. So soon after him sneering at what he saw as my mate's hair trigger for shifting.

"I'm serious, boy. Be careful with your choice of lifestyle. You end these shenanigans now, or you're no longer welcome. Not just in my home, but in my pack."

"Choice of lifestyle? Father... this is who I am. Who I've always been. It's where destiny has put me. This goes far beyond choice. You know how the mate bond works, after all."

"Mate? You're already mated?"

I faced him straight on, and opened my shirt, revealing the mark on my neck.

"Whose is that?"

Conall stepped forward. "It's mine."

EVIE RILEY

My father rolled his eyes and sneered. "Marking only happens between a man and a woman. That's not a true mark. We can still fix this."

This time it was Fiona who stepped in. "There is nothing here to *be* fixed, sir. Time moves on. Things change. Why, one day we might even end up with a female Alpha."

"And that's no doubt been your plan all along, hasn't it, you little bitch?"

My wolf came fully alive, as did Conall's. But if Fiona was bothered by father's insult, she never let on.

"My plan was to marry your son, and ease tensions between the packs. Circumstances changed. It's always been my belief that adaptability is not just a strength, but an absolutely vital survival mechanism."

HIS FATED MATE

Anton Valenta crossed his arms. "Last chance, boy. Think what you're throwing away."

I turned to Conall, finding strength and hope in nothing more than the light in his eyes. "I'm not throwing anything away, father. I'm just leaving it behind."

For a few more seconds, my father stood there, bristling. His voice was cold and quiet when he finally spoke again. "Then you will serve as an example to the rest of *my* people."

I heard, rather than saw, him leave. I only had eyes for Conall by that point.

This wasn't the way I'd wanted to tell him. There was still a huge part of me that insisted I should go to him, and fulfill the duty I was born into. That he'd drilled into me every day of my life.

But that would mean turning away

EVIE RILEY

from my future. The only future I had, or could want.

Life with Conall.

EPILOGUE

TWO YEARS LATER
CONALL

I WOULD NEVER tire of this. Waking up with Zoltan's hot, tight body snuggled up to mine was as important as the air I breathed.

From that aborted wedding day onward, he'd been an out and proud member of the Gray Vale pack, and neither of us had ever been happier.

His father turned out to be absolutely right when he said Zoltan would serve as an example to his people. But he could never have predicted exactly how.

When Anton went public with the details of Zoltan's excommunication, he'd unwittingly launched a revolution in Stoke Ridge. Dozens of previously secret same-sex couples were inspired to come out in support of the deposed son of their Alpha.

The shift was seismic, and in a last ditch effort to shore up his position, Anton Valenta had taken the clichéd old *if you're not with me you're against me* stand. Turned out, the majority was against him, and he vacated. Even Zee doesn't know where he's gone.

Though my mate was within his rights

to stand for the position, he'd shot that idea down in flames. That suited me just fine, since I'd come to feel exactly the same way about pack leadership. Now, we lived a life of blissful happiness and comfort, without the pressures and hassles that we were clearly unsuitable for.

In fact, we were only a week or so away from moving to a quiet cabin we'd had built right in the heart of the formerly disputed lands. A small place where we could hunt and garden, and raise some kids sometime in the future. A place we could grow old together.

The perfection of that idea hadn't waned one bit since Zee first suggested it. In the bliss of his warmth and his scent, I took a few seconds to gaze at his smooth and chiseled features, studying them as if they were new to me. As if I hadn't done exactly this, every morning for the past two years.

A few moments later he stirred, so I rolled him down onto his back and came up over the top of him. He opened his sweet, golden eyes to me, and I had to catch my breath.

The man was just so fucking beautiful.

He reached up and pressed his fingers to the side of my neck, right where he'd marked me. The exact same location as where I'd marked him first. I gasped when he pressed harder, and then let my body fall, taking his mouth in a deep kiss.

A light knocking on my apartment door cut through the moment. It seemed visitors were always interrupting us.

"Go away unless you have pizza," I yelled.

HIS FATED MATE

"I know you're a lazy ass, brother dear, but you haven't slept *that* long. It's not dinner time yet."

"Shit. It's the boss!"

Zee rolled his eyes at me, which only made me want to tackle him to the floor and make wild, lupine love to him. Of course, we were still sleeping off last night's crazy sex. That was the whole reason we were still in bed at... I glanced at the clock...holy fuck. 10:30?

I slid out of bed, fending off Zee's grabby hands as I pulled on a pair of track pants. I went through and opened the front door, firing my best cheeky grin at my sister.

"Why did you let me sleep so late, Fi?"

"You want the truth?"

"Of course not."

"Then, uh... let's see. Well, now that

EVIE RILEY

you're just a layabout loser with zero responsibilities—"

"Woah. That's the sugarcoated version? I mean, you're not wrong and all, but still..."

"Is my *other* brother in?"

I couldn't contain my broad grin. "Why do you think I'm sleeping so late?"

"Ugh. Keep it in your pants, bro." She called out to Zee, over my shoulder. "Other bro, time to dress up in your fancy duds."

"Oh, yeah," I murmured. "Today's the big day. The handing over of the royal staff and shit."

"I thought you'd already taken care of the *royal staff*. But we'll wake you when it's over, if you wanna grab your blankie and go back for a little nap time."

"Uh-uh. I'll be there, front and center.

You think I'm gonna miss out on seeing my little sister being anointed as the united packs' custodian? You'll even get to boss dad around."

"It's not that kind of situation, bro. You know that."

"Yeah. But you could come up with some way to make him squirm, surely."

"If I was gonna make anybody squirm, bro, you know it'd be you. But thank you for your support."

"No problem. And since it's a formal event, I'll bring my *black* whoopie cushion."

She shook her head. "Thanks again for reminding me of the bullet we all dodged when you stepped away, bro."

I pulled her into a tight hug. "Wrong, Fi. I didn't need to step away. You're the true Alpha, even if we're not calling it that anymore. You always were."

Zee came up behind and wrapped himself around my back, making sure to ruffle Fi's hair.

"God, you really *are* an extra brother now, aren't you?"

"Definitely. And I have a lot of years of annoying to catch up on."

She pushed away from us and tidied herself up again. "Well, you clearly have the best teacher."

I took a theatrical bow. "Thank you, oh Grand Poobah. I live to serve."

"Well, to dish it out, at least." My sister sighed heavily, a tiny grin forming on her lips. "You were bad enough when you had authority. Now... I think you're gonna put your back out from bucking the system."

"It'll be fine, sis."

"Oh?"

HIS FATED MATE

"Yeah." I put my arm over Zee's shoulder. "I have help."

Thank you for reading!

***

For more in the Gray Wolf Pack series to come in the future, follow me on all my social media channels.

***

For a Preview of Shattered, From The Edge, Book One, all you need to do is turn the page...

PREVIEW

Jimmy

The sound of the final bell going off had never sounded sweeter to me than right this moment. I had a love for school, but that last class in the day, political science, could really drag on for centuries. Some days, like today, it took all of my strength just to keep my eyes physically open. I quickly got the hell out of there

EVIE RILEY

and made my way toward my locker. Being eighteen and a senior in high school came with a good batch of mixed feelings. Sadness, because the school you had spent the past four years in, growing up in, was no longer going to be in your life. All of the teachers and friends you had made along the way weren't going to be sitting next to you at lunch or making you laugh in the library just to upset the world's crankiest librarian. It was a piece of your life that was finishing and it was bittersweet because your future was waiting for you right around the corner. For me, my future was waiting for me six blocks from here, at my part-time job.

I hastily said goodbye to the people I knew in the hallway as I made my way out of the building. I had to get to my work so I wouldn't be late. I had made a

HIS FATED MATE

habit of never being late for work and I was not about to start now.

Working at the diner wasn't fascinating, and it didn't help me with my art, but it paid me every two weeks and that money went toward art supplies and my savings for when I went off to college in the fall. Plus, working at the diner was not that bad. There were certainly worse part-time jobs I could be doing. In a city like Gaithersburg, Maryland you still had that small town feel, even though there was a decent size population, just under sixty thousand. Most would find that small, but when you think about how some cities only have a couple thousand people, I would say Gaithersburg was a decent size.

With that small town feel, though, you still had people with small town beliefs,

EVIE RILEY

like religion, politics, and sexual orientation. Two out of the three you could easily hide, but the sexual orientation part was a bit harder. Eventually, someone would notice you holding the hand of someone that was the same gender as you. Don't get me wrong, there were a lot of forward thinking people. A lot of accepting people who didn't care who you loved as long as you were happy. It was those people that got someone like me, a gay teenager, through the harder days.

My parents are some of those people. They are truly amazing. I'd been such a nervous wreck when I'd decided to come out to them when I was fourteen. I'd been terrified with how they would react. They'd always been supportive of me where my art was concerned, but I also knew it was one thing to accept that your son was never going to be a football player and another that he was gay. They had taken it like a dream.

I was all prepared for a big showdown. I'd practiced what I was going to say to them and I was prepared for any argument they were going to throw my way. All of my hard work was wasted when my mom just simply said they knew and asked what I wanted for dinner. I had gone in fully prepared that my parents were going to be shocked. Only for the tables to be turned, leaving me the one that was stunned stupid in the living room.

All of my stress and worrying had been for nothing, absolutely nothing. I was so shocked and ecstatic that I went to school the very next day and told my friend

EVIE RILEY

Danny all about it. He had wanted to tell his parents about being gay, but he was really worried with how religious they were. He finally told them earlier this year. Only it didn't go over so well.

He'd called me that night crying his eyes out because his parents had kicked him out. All he had left was his backpack and a single duffle bag with his clothes and personal belongings. They completely threw him out without even a second thought about where he would go. I had immediately told him to come to my house and my parents both agreed that he could stay with us if he couldn't stay with his older brother who had his own apartment in town.

Thankfully, Danny's brother was not a jerk and had been pissed at his parents for kicking out his kid brother. Danny moved in with him and never had to hide who he was again. Neither of them have spoken to their parents since that night and I doubted they ever would.

That night, though, gave me a whole new level of respect for Danny. He had shown some true courage to tell his parents and then when they forced him to leave, he didn't try and put the genie back into the bottle. He held his head up high and became a proud gay kid. It was only proof to how strong he was and I couldn't have been more proud of him.

The aroma of the diner welcomed me as I stepped through the door for my shift. Most would find it gross, I suppose, but to me it smelled like the fifties. I can't explain it, but the odor from the grill with the eggs, the sweet sugar smell of waffles, the rich scent of brewed coffee, it always reminded me of poodle skirts and really bad hairstyles. I

t didn't look like the fifties, but the Main Street Diner had been here since then. The one wall to the left of the diner was covered in photos from the past eight decades. They weren't organized at all, either, just thrown up where there was a spot. The owner, Anthony Blackstone, had taken over the diner from his father. It had been in their generation since the very first day. They were a pillar in the community and everyone still came here, even with some of the National chain restaurants just down the street. You just couldn't beat the food here, especially for breakfast.

"Hey, Sal, how are you?" I called to one of my regulars.

HIS FATED MATE

He was a very sweet seventy-year-old man who used to come here with his wife. They had been married for forty years before he lost her to cancer two years ago. They used to come here every Thursday night to have date night. They had their first date right here in the diner almost fifty years ago. Every Thursday, they would come in and sit in the same booth every single time. We would make sure no one sat in it before they had the chance to get here.

Sal had been coming here after her death, still. He would sit in the same spot and place her framed photograph across from him. It sounded really sad, I know, but to him it was his way of still having their date night together.

He once told me that there were many days where he missed her so much it hurt, but when he came to the diner for their date night, he felt connected to her. The pain didn't hurt so much and he truly believed that she was sitting in that booth seat right across from him. It was the sweetest thing I had ever heard, still to this day.

I didn't know if I believed in spirits or not, but what I did know is that I hoped it was true. I hoped that Martha was sitting right there in that booth with Sal, spending time together until they could be reunited again.

"I'm still moving, Jim," Sal said, flashing a toothless grin.

"I'm happy to hear that. This place wouldn't be the same without you, Sal."

I made my way toward the back room so I could drop my coat and bag off. I was hoping it might be a little dead tonight so

HIS FATED MATE

I could get a jump start on my homework. Dead was never good for tips, but it did allow me to get my homework done before getting home, allowing me the time to relax and watch a couple episodes of my favorite show before I would have to go to sleep.

After clocking in, I made my way behind the counter and gave Stella a big smile. "Hey good looking, how's it been?" I asked.

In her thirties now, Stella had been working here for ten years. She'd dropped out of high school at sixteen when she got pregnant. Her boyfriend at the time was a high school senior and he took off right after graduation before their daughter was even born. She came from a single mother, who kicked her out once she discovered that she was pregnant. Stella didn't let it get to her, though. She persevered and she created a life for her daughter. She had been working odd jobs for the first four years before she was given the opportunity to work here full-time. Mr. Blackstone was really good with her and even gave her health benefits for her daughter after she had worked here for six months. Stella had been eternally grateful to Mr. Blackstone and as a result, she always came into work and even worked extra shifts if they had no one to cover. She was a hard and loyal worker and I loved her from the first day we met.

"Not too bad, Jimmy. You know how Thursdays are. How was school?"

"It was uneventful, which is exactly how I like it. I have some homework, but if it's dead in here later I can always work on it."

HIS FATED MATE

"You must be getting excited with graduation creeping up," Stella said flashing a warm smile.

"I guess I am. I don't know, it doesn't feel real yet. Maybe it would be different if I was going to travel the world or move to a completely different State. But to me, it just feels like I'm going to school in the fall. Only this one will be like a boarding school that I get to come home for on weekends," I said with a shrug.

"Don't worry about that too much. It will feel more real once you are living in the dorms. Then, in your second year, you'll be getting your own place. It'll sink in once you're there and taking classes."

That sounded about right. I wasn't the type of person who got excited to begin with, really. Of course, I was looking

EVIE RILEY

forward to it, but I wasn't jumping up and down with excitement.

Before anymore could be said, the little bell above the door chimed and we both looked up, expecting to be greeting a customer. Instead, we saw our new manager walking in.

We had been told a few days ago that we would be getting a new night manager. Stella had been offered the job, but she liked being a server. She liked the lack of responsibility more than anything. She said she had enough going on with raising a teenager; she didn't need more of a headache. She was open to the idea at a later time, though, when her daughter was off to College herself.

I had been prepared for the new manager to be someone like the old manager, Mr. Wilson, older and not really attractive. This man, though, he was nothing like I was expecting.

He had short brown hair; much like myself only mine was blonde. He had a clear five o'clock shadow that he had no interest in trying to get rid of, which was fine by me. I liked a man that looked a bit rough. He was well built, like he spent some time working out at the gym in his day, but he wasn't so muscular that it was the only thing he did in the day. He walked with his head held up high and his back straight.

He didn't appear to be nervous at all for someone starting a new job. He glanced over at us and I felt a quick, warm shot of arousal at seeing his emerald green eyes. It was only for a moment before he was heading into the back, but I could have sworn he had mesmerized me with them. I couldn't take my eyes off of him, even after he had disappeared into the kitchen area. My gaze lingered on the door, hoping he would come back out.

"Earth to Jimmy, come back, you're drooling," Stella teased.

"I don't drool," I said, feeling my cheeks warm as I forced myself to look back over to her.

That granted me a chuckle. "Man, if I knew the new manager was going to look like that, I would have worn tighter pants." Stella winked.

"I think I should have worn looser ones," I joked back. But in all honesty, getting a hard-on at work was not a good idea. Thankfully, I had a server's apron on that would hide any issues should something get out of control. And by something, I mean my imagination. Hey, I was an artist; I had a remarkable imagination.

One that had gotten me through many lonely nights.

"You're so bad. What do you think, straight or gay?"

"You know, most people worry if their new boss is going to be a dick or not. Not what team they play for," I said with a playful smirk as I leaned my left side against the counter. I was not going to admit out loud that I was wondering the exact same thing.

And praying it was the latter.

"I doubt he's a dick. He doesn't look old enough to be a dick. He's like twenty, maybe twenty-one. And I'm allowed to wonder all I want. I'm just not allowed to ask. I'm going with straight, though. He's got that straight boy look."

"Can't argue with that. He's very pretty, though."

He was most likely straight. Odds were in his favor for being straight, but that didn't mean I couldn't window shop to my heart's content. I didn't have much time to ponder my new boss, because a table of four teenagers walked through the door. I went back to focusing on my work. Whatever was going to happen with our new manager would happen regardless of what I wanted. For now, I would wait until I would get to be introduced.

***

It was a good two hours later when I had a moment to catch my breath. The dinner rush had come through and it was always

HIS FATED MATE

busy for a few hours before everyone started to head out for home. Then only a few stragglers would come in for a late dessert or a coffee before they got back on the road. While I was in the middle of filling the napkin dispensers once again, Mr. Wilson made his way out of the kitchen with the new manager.

"Jimmy, meet our new night manager, Zane Hamilton," Mr. Wilson said.

Zane.

The name suited him. Strong, masculine, but unique. It wasn't a name you heard every day in your life. Seeing Zane up close like this only allowed me to realize that he looked even more sexy up close and personal than he did from a distance.

His eyes were to die for. I had never seen eyes this green before. He had a strong jaw and chiseled facial features that gave him a model like look. He was truly breath-stealing to look at up close. This man was a heartbreaker and I had no doubt that he would have a trail of hopeful lovers behind him.

I sighed inwardly, knowing working for this sexy-as-sin man would be a challenge of the worst kind on my active imagination.

"Hi, it's nice to meet you, Sir," I said, trying to remember that this was my boss and I needed to be polite and friendly. I was leaving for College come the fall, but I needed this job to make sure I could have enough saved up until I found a job up there.

"Call me Zane, please." His voice held a slight gravelly tone to it, but it wasn't from something like smoking. It was completely natural and it sent a shiver right down my spine.

"Well, it's nice to meet you, Zane. I'm sure you will love working here, the customers are great and the other employees are really friendly. If you have any questions, don't be afraid to ask."

God, yes, please ask me anything you want.

I would love to talk with him for my whole shift. Anything that would allow me to get close to him. I bet he smelled amazing.

"Thank you, I appreciate that. I'm sure I will love working here."

I knew *I* was going to love him working here. This job just got so much better. I couldn't stand around and talk, though, because I had a new table come in and

EVIE RILEY

the last thing I wanted to do was leave a bad impression on my new boss.

I sighed, made my excuses, and quickly headed back to work, waving goodbye to Mr. Wilson as he headed out. I did my best to focus on my work, but I could feel eyes on me. Zane's eyes. I knew it without even having to look at him.

I didn't have a problem being watched. I mean, it's common when you get a new boss. A good manager would always look around, check out how you work and what habits you had, or even what routine there already was in place. So Zane watching me throughout my shift wasn't that out of the norm.

The thing was, though, he wasn't looking at me like he was evaluating my skills. He was just following me around with his eyes. It was a little awkward and it left me feeling a bit weirded out by it. That was, until I saw just the slightest glimmer of what could only be described as lust in his eyes when I bent over the table to wipe the far end of it. I looked up just in time for him to snap his eyes away and look over at another customer.

Oh my god!

Is he checking me out?

That couldn't be right, right?

There was no way that he would be checking me out. Even if he was interested in guys, why would he be interested in someone like me? I couldn't be his type. As badly as I wished I was his type. Guys like him wouldn't go for the artistic type like me. I had enough experience in my dating life to know that.

Still, though, the thought of him checking me out didn't leave me feeling awkward or creeped out. It left me feeling a tingle of excitement. I knew nothing could come from it and I was perfectly okay with that.

One thing I did know, work was going to be so much more enjoyable.

For more of Shattered, From The Edge, Book One, check out your favorite online retailer!

OTHER BOOKS BY EVIE

Federal Protection Agency
Mason
Rafe
Ryzen
Cooper
Noah
Damien
Sebastian
Gabe
Logan

Ruthless Empire
Courting Danger
Chasing Danger
Kissing Danger

Smokejumpers
Hawke
Cyrus
Jase
Gage
Jackson
Xavier

Jasper Springs
Cade
Dawson
Drew
Grayson
Riley
Mitch

From The Edge
Shattered
Runaway
Jaded
Rescue
Hidden
Tormented

Gray Vale Pack
His Fated Mate
His Wounded Warrior
His Healing Heart

ABOUT THE AUTHOR

Evie Riley is a prolific, neurodivergent author known for her captivating MM romance novels. She has gained a significant following and topped the LGBT+ action and adventure bestseller charts with her series.

Evie's writing style often explores dark and gritty themes where her men must overcome difficult obstacles in their search for love, but she has also ventured into sweeter small-town romances, incorporating tropes like enemies-to-lovers, friends-to-lovers, age-gap, and forced proximity. She is known for crafting engaging romantic suspense novels and has a knack for creating interconnected series worlds that keep readers invested.

EVIE RILEY

Interestingly, Ms. Riley has hinted at exploring new genres, such as Alien Omegaverse Romance, in the future.

Outside of writing, she enjoys spending time at the beach and has a quirky personality, described by her partner as ranging from cute to deadly, depending on her blood-chocolate levels.

Evie spends her nights writing bad boys in love, and her days wrangling the sweet boys she loves.